NATASHA WING'S
The Night Before
Halloween
ACTIVITY BOOK

By Natasha Wing

Art by Cynthia Fisher

Grosset & Dunlap

For Dan, my Halloween partner—NW

For Kiera and Rory, all grown up now—CF

GROSSET & DUNLAP
An Imprint of Penguin Random House LLC, New York

Text copyright © 2020 by Natasha Wing. Illustrations copyright © 2020 by Penguin Random House LLC. All rights reserved.
Published by Grosset & Dunlap, an imprint of Penguin Random House LLC, New York.
GROSSET & DUNLAP is a registered trademark of Penguin Random House LLC. Manufactured in China.

Visit us online at www.penguinrandomhouse.com.

ISBN 9780593095584   10 9 8 7 6 5 4 3 2 1

In *The Night Before Halloween*, monsters prepare their haunted house for the biggest holiday of the year— Halloween! Kids are getting into the Halloween spirit, too, with parades, costumes, and hayrides.

But when the children go trick-or-treating and knock on the haunted house door, they're in for a spine-tingling thrill!

These activities offer fun ways to get ready for your *own* magical Halloween night.

Hide-and-Seek

There are six Halloween-related words hidden in this puzzle.
Circle them if you can find them!

spooky	candy	mask
pumpkin	witch	skeleton

T	J	T	V	N	U	T	M	J	I
W	I	S	K	E	L	E	T	O	N
I	F	D	H	S	Q	N	H	Z	X
T	H	E	P	E	P	R	D	T	C
C	C	W	U	G	S	O	V	C	E
H	A	X	M	W	H	R	O	Y	V
B	N	M	P	Q	S	B	L	K	B
Y	D	A	K	W	K	Q	J	O	Y
L	Y	S	I	G	L	K	V	X	W
Q	I	K	N	A	Y	Q	E	R	N

4

A Ghost Out of Thin Air

Watch a white ghost appear before your eyes!

Stare at the center of the black ghost and slowly count to twenty. Then look at a black surface (a black piece of paper or even a computer monitor screen that is turned off can work) and relax your eyes. What do you see appear out of thin air?

Trick-or-Treat!

These trick-or-treaters are going from house to house collecting candy. But when they get to the last house on the street, they discover it might be haunted!

Are you brave enough to knock on the door? Start at the house on the top left, then see if you can find your way to the haunted house on the hill.

Start

End

Fright Night, Flight Night

With a black crayon or marker, color in the shapes that contain a dot to find out what's flying around in the dark.

8

Kooky Spooky

On Halloween night, things can get a little weird.
Can you spot what's wrong with this picture?

Mystery Mask

Connect the dots and reveal who is smiling back at you.

Boo-nana Milkshake

The witches are throwing a Halloween party for their monster friends and are serving boo-nana milkshakes. Here's the spook-tacular recipe that you and an adult can make and serve at your party.

Ingredients:

1 banana

1 cup milk

¼ cup Greek yogurt

1 tablespoon oats

honey to taste (optional)

To decorate:

glass bottle or drinking glass

googly eyes

glue stick

marker

1. Peel the banana and ask an adult to slice it into circles. Then lay them out on a lined baking tray and freeze for a couple of hours or overnight.

2. Decorate the bottle or drinking glass by gluing on two googly eyes and drawing on a mouth with marker.

3. Add the milk, Greek yogurt, oats, and frozen banana slices to a blender. Ask an adult to help you blend the mixture until completely smooth, then taste and add a little honey to sweeten, if needed.

4. Pour the drink into your prepared bottle or glass and serve immediately.

Halloween Costume Parade

Can you find the objects hiding in this picture?

- ☐ cat
- ☐ broom
- ☐ bat
- ☐ jack-o'-lantern
- ☑ flashlight   ☐ skeleton bone
- ☐ mask   ☐ tombstone
- ☐ witch's hat   ☐ mummy

Black Cat Magic

This white kitty has a secret. On Halloween night, it changes color.

Stare at the nose of the white kitty and slowly count to twenty.
Then look at a white piece of paper. Meow! What color cat do you see ?

Candy Trail

Poor Frankenstein had a hole in his trick-or-treat bag. Start at the house at the top of the page and follow the trail that Frankenstein took. How many candies did he drop?

Pumpkin Pairs

When you hollow them out, carve them, and then place a light inside, pumpkins become jack-o'-lanterns that glow in the night.

Draw a line from each jack-o'-lantern on the top to the matching jack-o'-lantern on the bottom.

Magical Potion

On the eve of Halloween, the witches brew up a magical potion that sets every monster and goblin in motion to help decorate the haunted house. Use the words below the symbols on this page to fill in the blank spaces on the next page. Make sure the symbol above the word you choose matches the symbol under the blank space. When you are done, you or an adult can read your story aloud!

NOUNS	ADJECTIVES	VERBS
toothbrush	slimy	wiggle
pizza	screaming	bounce
beanbag	bloody	gag
bathtub	smelly	hiccup
firecracker	green	spin

On the night of a full moon, the witches gathered around a _____ with their friends.

Tonight they would make a magical potion. "What do we need?" asked the _____ goblin.

"First, we toss a _____ into a boiling pot of pond water. Then we add a scoop of

crushed bugs. When the pot starts to _____ , we stir in a _____ .

And lastly, we sprinkle in _____ red beets."

Count Dracula scooped up a spoonful of the _____ potion. "Don't swallow that!"

said the old witch. "You'll turn into a _____ ."

He started to _____ . Then he yelled, "Smorgle-dee-pancakes!" Suddenly he ran

off into the night.

"It's ready," said the old witch with a grin.

Zombie Crawl

The zombie is looking for something to eat.
Help him get through the maze so he can reach the sweet treat.
Avoid the trees and spiderwebs!

Howl-o-ween

Who's that howling at the moon? Connect the dots to find out.

Vanishing Words

Six words have disappeared into the puzzle below!
Can you find them? Circle these words when you do.

| pirate | mummy | ghost |
| parade | monster | Halloween |

Z	P	I	R	A	T	E	E	N	P
U	A	K	M	X	T	V	D	N	T
V	H	A	L	L	O	W	E	E	N
N	U	B	C	Y	T	R	U	G	H
K	I	M	Z	H	P	A	M	C	V
W	G	U	M	O	N	S	T	E	R
T	H	M	P	P	U	A	P	L	C
Q	O	M	P	W	W	B	Y	I	V
G	S	Y	T	Y	Q	P	P	P	J
F	T	P	A	R	A	D	E	D	O

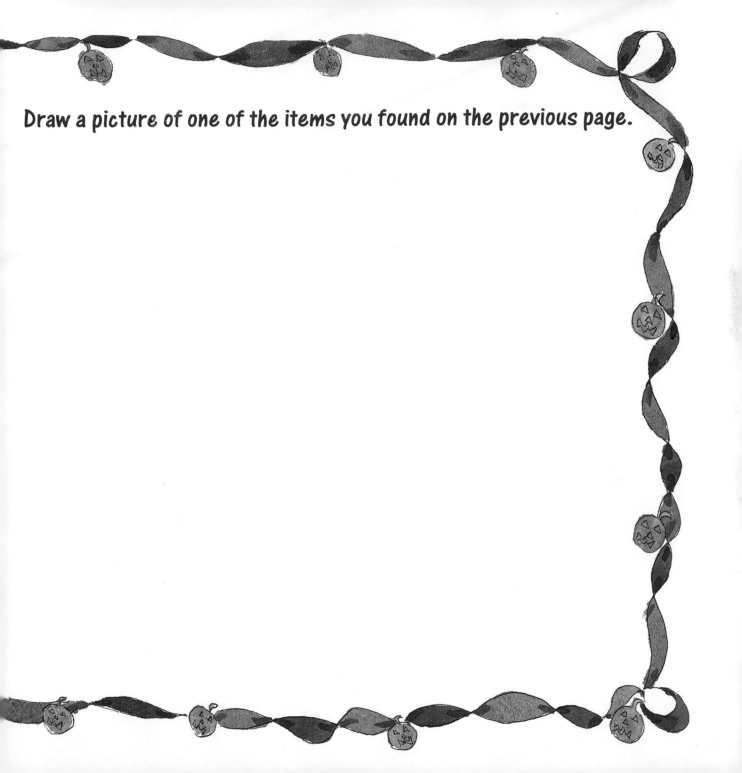

Draw a picture of one of the items you found on the previous page.

Answer Key

Page 4

T	J	T	V	N	U	T	M	J	I
W	I	S	K	E	L	E	T	O	N
I	F	D	H	S	Q	N	H	Z	X
T	H	E	P	E	P	R	D	T	C
C	C	W	U	G	S	O	V	C	E
H	A	X	M	W	H	R	O	Y	V
B	N	M	P	Q	S	B	L	K	B
Y	D	A	K	W	K	Q	J	O	Y
L	Y	S	I	G	L	K	V	X	W
Q	I	K	N	A	Y	Q	E	R	N

Page 7

Page 8

Page 9

Page 10

11
12
10
13
9
7
18
17
16
14
8
15
19
6
20
5
68
70
69
31
32
66 67
21
4
72
71
65
64 33 34
22
73
62 36 35
29
63 54 37 38 39 30
28
60
61
23
59 55 40 41
3
75
57 53 43 42
26 27
58 49
45 24
74
50 56 52 46
2
1 48
51 44 25
76
18
47
77

Page 12

Page 14

Frankenstein dropped 8 pieces of candy on the trail!

Page 15

Page 18

Page 19

Page 20

Z	P	I	R	A	T	E	E	N	P
U	A	K	M	X	T	V	D	N	T
V	H	A	L	L	O	W	E	E	N
N	U	B	C	Y	T	R	U	G	H
K	I	M	Z	H	P	A	M	C	V
W	G	U	M	O	N	S	T	E	R
T	H	M	P	P	U	A	P	L	C
Q	O	M	P	W	W	B	Y	I	V
G	S	Y	T	Y	Q	P	P	P	J
F	T	P	A	R	A	D	E	D	O